# Big Dog, Little Dog

## P. D. Eastman

www.randomhouse.com/kids

*Library of Congress Cataloging-in-Publication Data*
Eastman, P. D. (Philip D.) Big dog . . . little dog / P. D. Eastman.  p.  cm. — "B-92."
SUMMARY: Two dogs are opposite in every way but are the very best of friends.
ISBN 0-375-82297-6 (trade) — ISBN 0-375-92297-0 (lib. bdg.)
[1. Dogs—Fiction. 2. Friendship—Fiction.]  I. Title.  PZ7.E1314 Bi 2003  [E]—dc21  2002151045

Printed in the United States of America  2003  18

# Big Dog...
## Little Dog

by P. D. Eastman

BEGINNER BOOKS®

A Division of Random House, Inc.

Fred and Ted were friends.

Fred was big.

Ted was little.

Fred always had money.

Ted never had money.

When they walked in the rain,

Fred was wet . . .

and Ted was dry.

They both liked music.

Fred played
the flute.

Ted played
the tuba.

When they had dinner,

Fred ate the spinach . . .

and Ted ate the beets.

When they painted the house,

Fred used green paint.

Ted used red.

One day Fred and Ted
went away in their cars.

Fred went in
his green car.

Ted went in
his red car.

Fred drove his car slowly.

Ted drove his car fast.

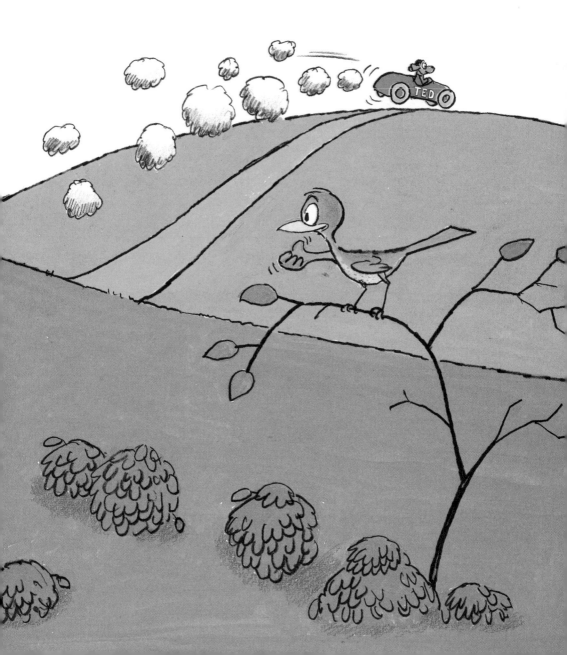

They came to a sign.

"Where should we go?" asked Fred.

"To the mountains," said Ted.

When they got to the mountains,

Ted skied all day long.

Fred skated all day long.

When they stopped,

Fred was cold.

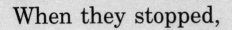

Ted was warm.

By night both of them
were very sleepy.
"Look!" said Fred.
"A small hotel!"

Fred's room was upstairs.

Ted's room was downstairs.

"Good night, Ted.
Sleep well," said Fred.

"Good night, Fred.
Sleep well," said Ted.

But they did *not* sleep well.

Upstairs, Fred thumped and bumped
and tossed and turned.

Downstairs, Ted moaned and groaned
and crashed and thrashed all over the bed.

When morning came,
Fred called Ted.

"Let's take a walk,"
Fred said to Ted.

"We can walk
and talk," said Ted
to Fred.

They walked uphill.

They walked downhill.

They made tall talk.

They made small talk.

"My bed is too little!"

"My bed is too big!"

"What can we do about it, Ted?"

"I don't know, Fred."

"I know what to do!"
said the bird.
"Ted should sleep upstairs
and Fred should sleep
downstairs!"

"The bird's got the word."

"Back to bed!"
yelled Ted.

"Back to bed!"
yelled Fred.

"It's downstairs for me!"
yelled Fred.

"It's upstairs for me!"
yelled Ted.

Ted jumped into
the little bed upstairs.

And Fred jumped into
the big bed downstairs.

Ted slept all day long
in the cozy little bed.

And Fred slept all day long
in the cozy big bed.

"Well, that was easy to do.
Big dogs need big beds.
Little dogs need little beds.
Why make big problems
out of little problems?"